A Visit to the Zoo

Celeste Bishop

illustrated by
Aurora Aguilera

PowerKiDS press.

New York

Published in 2017 by The Rosen Publishing Group, Inc.
29 East 21st Street, New York, NY 10010

First Edition

Managing Editor: Nathalie Beullens-Maoui
Editor: Theresa Morlock
Book Design: Mickey Harmon
Illustrator: Aurora Aguilera

Library of Congress Cataloging-in-Publication Data

Names: Bishop, Celeste, author.
Title: A visit to the zoo / Celeste Bishop.
Description: New York : PowerKids Press, [2017] | Series: Places in my
   community | Includes index.
Identifiers: LCCN 2016027643| ISBN 9781499427721 (pbk. book) | ISBN
   9781508152880 (6 pack) | ISBN 9781499430189 (library bound book)
Subjects: LCSH: Zoos–Juvenile literature. | Zoo animals–Juvenile literature.
Classification: LCC QL76 .B57 2017 | DDC 590.73–dc23
LC record available at https://lccn.loc.gov/2016027643

Manufactured in the United States of America

CPSIA Compliance Information: Batch #BW17PK: For Further Information contact Rosen Publishing, New York, New York at 1-800-237-9932

Contents

My mom is taking me
to the zoo today!

A zoo is a place where
animals live.

Some of the animals are
from faraway places.

8

Zoos have big animals and small animals. I like to see them all.

They have a pool to swim in.

12

After the penguins, we see the elephants.
Their long nose is called a trunk.

Our next stop is the lion house.

Lions have a furry head and sharp teeth.
Roar!

It's time for the sea lion show!

They do lots of tricks.

18

People who work at the zoo
are called zookeepers.
They take good care
of the animals.

We have time to visit one more animal.

We see the monkeys. They're silly!

Soon it's time to leave.

The zoo is one of my favorite places.

23

Words to Know

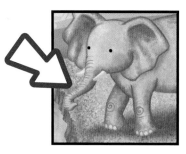

penguin   trunk   zookeeper

Index